e-smuggler.com

by Sedef Ecer

translated by Amelia Parenteau

NoPassport Press

e-smuggler.com

by Sedef Ecer

translated by Amelia Parenteau

NoPassport Press Dreaming the Americas Series
NoPassport Press, PO Box 1786, South Gate, CA 90280 USA; e-mail: NoPassportPress@aol.com; website: www.nopassport.org

ISBN: 978-1-79476-211-4

e-smuggler.com

by Sedef Ecer

was translated by Amelia Parenteau with support from

About the Translator and Author

Amelia Parenteau is a writer, translator, and theater maker based in New Orleans. An alumna of Sarah Lawrence College, she has worked with TCG, Ping Chong + Company, The Lark, The Civilians, the French Institute Alliance Française, Voyage Theater Company, and The Park Avenue Armory in New York; People's Light in Pennsylvania; and the Eugene O'Neill Theater Center in Connecticut. She is a member of the FENCE International Translation Network and ATLAS. She has translated plays by the Théâtre du Soleil, Sedef Ecer, Alain Foix, Leslie Kaplan, David Lescot, and Charlotte Boimare & Magali Solignat. Publications include: *American Theatre Magazine, Asymptote, Contemporary Theatre Review, Culturebot, HowlRound,* and *Stain'd.*

Born in Istanbul, **Sedef Ecer** grew up in the world of movie-making, theater and television. She has acted in 25 feature films and several plays since she was three years old, and has recently worked under the direction of Amos Gitaï (with Jeanne Moreau), Lorenzo Gabriel, Thomas Bellorini, etc. Her plays have been directed by Elise Chatauret, Thomas Bellorini, Bruno Freyssinet, Vincent Goethals, Tina Brueggemann, Hansguenther Heyme, Lisa Rothe, Evren Odcikin, Shiva Ordooi, and many others. As a writer and actress, she has been a nominee or a recipient of prestigious awards. She writes different genres and in two languages – she has written more than 500 articles or opinion pieces for the press, novels, screenplays, explored new genres and translated Montaigne, Charlotte Delbo, and Saint-Exupery's works into Turkish – but her major work is in the field of theater. Her plays are performed in numerous theaters and festivals in different countries, published by Les Éditions de l'Amandier, Les Éditions l'Espace d'un Instant, Lansman and l'Avant-Scène in France, and translated into Polish, Turkish, Armenian, German, Greek, English, Persian, Italian etc. A staged reading of her play *e-smuggler.com*, translated by Amelia Parenteau, directed by Lisa Rothe, and produced by Voyage Theater Company, was presented at the New York Public Library in October 2018. The season of Crowded Fire Theatre in San Francisco, CA will begin with the American premiere of Sedef Ecer's *At the Periphery* (Feb. 23-April 4), translated from the Turkish by Evren Odcikin. Ecer's play follows the lives of two generations of migrants in urban Istanbul. Crowded Fire will present *At the Periphery* in co-production with Golden Thread Productions in San Francisco. Erin Gilley will direct.

About *e-smuggler.com*

It's the end of the United Nations. Countries no longer
exist, and all world citizens have become nomadic
refugees, avoiding conflicts and ecological catastrophes.
The only real power now rests in the hands of a
smuggler who, through his cell phone, surveils borders
that are redrawn daily. As for the refugees, nothing
is left but their smartphones as a link to the world: they
contact their smuggler via Whatsapp, find their way
thanks to Google Maps, talk to their family by Skype, keep
informed of the dangers awaiting them through
Facebook groups, and follow political changes in their
home countries over Twitter, all of which leaves a
digital footprint everywhere they go. When the refugees
traverse land and sea, the virtual smuggler shows
them the way.

Among these thousands of digital nomads, the audience
follows three women through their cyberidentities.
Anaba the midwife heads to San Francisco, leaving behind
her dispensary project and her native village, where the
Mayan population is being oppressed. Hoa Mi leaves for
Paris, following a digital lover. And Zeynab sets off
pregnant, while her husband, an archeologist like her,
stays behind to protect the sarcophagus of a young girl
who was sacrificed before the barbarians arrived. The final
scene takes place on a train where the three women meet
as Zeynab gives birth.

e-smuggler.com was written in Turkish (2015) and French (2016) versions by Sedef Ecer, and translated
from the French by Amelia Parenteau with support from France's Centre National du Livre. Ecer and
Parenteau worked to refine the translation in residency at The Lark in New York City, culminating in a
staged reading at the New York Public Library in 2018, presented by Voyage Theater Company (Wayne Maugans, Artistic Director) and directed by Lisa Rothe.

Characters

E-SMUGGLER: strange character with an intoxicating manner of speech. Chic Mafioso? Spider-Man? Joker? Kitschy reality TV host? Mechanical traveling salesman? Matrix acrobat?

ANABA: a Guatemalan midwife
HOA MI: a Vietnamese hairdresser
ZEYNAB: a Syrian archeologist
(These three women can be played by one or three actresses.)

THE PERCUSSIONIST: a virtual double, sometimes a voice double, sometimes a virtual being, and sometimes off-stage characters. Virtuosic multi-instrumentalist.

Setting

An upstage screen used to alternate pre-recorded images with live stream: Instagram photos, videos, Facebook statuses, WhatsApp chats, Twitter feeds, Skype windows, smartphone applications, all digital elements, reworked and stylized. (These images do not illustrate what happens on stage.)

The set is composed of these projected images and several long strings, which E-SMUGGLER uses to gradually surround the stage and a few of the audience's seats. He outlines new frontiers, creates social networks, and connects us – audience and actors – using the strings. A 16-meter red trapeze silk cloth serves as a swing, house, country, boat, sea, and street.

Music

The percussion belongs to E-SMUGGLER's world. Each woman's world contains a song (Latin American for ANABA, Asian for HOA MI, and an Arab elegy for ZEYNAB).

"Since the beginning of the 'migrant and refugee crisis,' we have sunk very deep into indifference. I've tried to imagine a story that goes even deeper." – Sedef Ecer

While the audience is settling in, we see a United Nations spokesperson appear on the screen.

UNITED NATIONS SPOKESPERSON: Ladies and gentlemen, I regret to inform you of the end of the United Nations, founded in 1945, which assembles all the world's countries. Starting today, the United Nations can no longer assure its objectives; namely, cooperation, international security, economic development, social progress, human rights, and world peace, because corporations are stronger than countries, and countries henceforth no longer exist. All wealth as well as property are now shared by 1% of the population. 99% have become nomadic refugees, who roam constantly due to conflicts and ecological catastrophes. Nations no longer exist, borders no longer exist. The extinction of the human race is predicted to occur in the next three generations. Climatologists are observing a constant temperature increase, and sea level is rising non-stop. To serve our needs, two planets are now necessary. We are no longer able to identify the armed conflicts in the world because the number changes every day. Progress in robotics and artificial intelligence has transformed the world of work, and connected devices have taken the place of humans. Henceforth, it's a match without a referee. Nothing is left but your cell phones. Consequently, in the name of the United Nations, I bid you adieu. No governments are left, no statesmen. Only He is left. E-smuggler.com.

THE PERCUSSIONIST begins to play. On the screen, E-SMUGGLER gets ready live in the dressing rooms. (This image can be pre-recorded but it should give the impression of being live.) Then a cameraperson follows E-SMUGGLER from the dressing room (Steadicam-style image), and we see him walk through backstage, and stop just before going on stage. Percussion. The camera continues to film E-SMUGGLER in close-up as he nervously waits for his entrance. Then suddenly, he has his TV host smile. Clean break, complete mood swing, he's about to go on. He enters.

E-SMUGGLER: Day and night, you are practically two billion people connecting to my site through your cell phone screens. You travel with me and you're right to do so, because e-smuggler.com, it's the future of our planet, and it's a future we're building together! *(Percussion.)* My dear wanderers, you thought it was over, you thought it couldn't continue, you thought it would stop there, you told yourself:

THE PERCUSSIONIST: *(with a vertiginous delivery, all rhythm, not always intelligible)* after this flux — there won't be more — after this war — there won't be more — the directors — these people in power — these finance bosses — these industrialists — they will stop this — this will end well one day — we can't go on like this — these autocrats — these warriors — these savages — these dictators — we'll overthrow them — the people will take charge of their destiny — these big movements — this will change our race — no, no, race no longer exists — anthropologists say so — but this will change our culture — our religion — no one cares about religion but our way of life — so this will stop — before all cafeterias become halal — allah u akbar — our roots are Christian — minarets everywhere…

E-SMUGGLER: But no, this won't stop. There will always be more. There will always be others. Migrants. Political refugees, economic, ecological. And who knows? You yourselves, maybe you will be forced to leave, whether you're rich or poor. Because there's no longer, like before, "them, there where they live, far away, over there," and then, "us, here where we live, here, here at home right here." No! We will be more and more mixed together. Our flesh, our blood, our languages, our religions, our habits will all become one. When you say, "go back home" to someone, it will no longer mean anything. It would have been very practical, "your home" and "my home," very well then, "our home," but no. When you say, "your home," that "your home" will be all of your homes and by the same token, "all of your homes" will be "their homes." You just have to accept this fact because you can't change it, and it won't do any good to fight. Either you'll flee, or you'll flee those who are fleeing.

THE PERCUSSIONIST: Some flee wars, earthquakes, floods, droughts, famines, diarrhea, hurricanes, deserts, conflicts, and others flee those who flee. You will either belong to one group or the other. You will be a wanderer among the wanderers and you will only have one weapon, your cell phone screen!

Percussion, then a sharp silence.

E-SMUGGLER: I remember my very first job, I must have been 15 years old. I had smuggled a three-person family across the border. Actually, no, they were four. A pregnant woman, her husband, and their son. That day, I said to myself that that was it, exactly what I wanted to do. We were living in a valley. My parents had built a small house, without knowing it, directly on a border. Half of the property was in one country, and the other half in another. My room, and that's not all, even my bed were literally on the line! When I slept, the left half of my body belonged to one country, and the right half belonged to the other. Like the children of musicians who naturally have an ear, or the children of masons who are good with their hands, or the children of chefs gifted with flavors, I was a child of the border, I had the demarcation written in me. My whole body became a border. I therefore developed this love of lines, of borders, of edges, thresholds, barriers, delimitations, separations, of demarcations, and I made my career out of them! I told myself…by smuggling people over the border, every day, I will make millions of people happy. I knew that I was going to make my career out of it, but how could I have guessed, at the time, that the entire global population would be transformed into wandering refugees, and that I would become the Lord of the Borders!

Percussion and again the "show!"

THE PERCUSSIONIST: Dear e-refugee, thank you for having selected us. Before leaving your country, you were a lawyer, a student, an architect, a florist, a doctor, and you will soon find yourself without anything on the road, you will suffer hunger, thirst, and cold, crossing land and sea.

E-SMUGGLER: But now, thanks to e-smuggler.com, you have a true traveling companion. You no longer need to find dishonest smugglers in each country you travel through, since we will stay in touch throughout your trek. You will be able to send me WhatsApp messages, speak to your family by Skype, read tweets from other migrants, navigate and find your way through Google Maps, look at photos on Instagram, and like our posts regularly on Facebook!

THE PERCUSSIONIST: With your smartphone, you will be able to reserve your place on a fishing boat, in a refrigerated truck, or on a container ship, book a mattress in a homeless camp, and still post selfies, all while crossing deadly borders. You will also be able to benefit from our advice by clicking on our "Daily Life" guide: how to slip in between the trailer and the cabin of an 18-wheeler, and how to erase your fingerprints by burning them off with acid, or by pulling the skin off your fingers. Our algorithms work day and night to create new services for you, and also to protect your data… Don't forget, the biggest name in the history of technology was the son of a Syrian refugee: Steve Jobs. Join today at e-smuggler.com!

Jingle.

E-SMUGGLER: What could be better than studying the smartphones of those whom I accompanied along their treks? What could be more instructive than entering into the virtual lives of those who wandered? A Turkish girl who's the victim of an arranged marriage, an oppressed Mayan woman from Guatemala, a Bangladeshi man chased out by rising sea levels, a Moroccan drag queen fleeing transphobia, all of them have a reason to leave, leaving us a shapeless mass of digital data. And I, Big Brother of two billion migrants, I like to follow your tracks, which make millions of gigabytes. I like to scrutinize your virtual identities, I like to examine your digital doubles, I like to dissect your two billion cell phones that I keep in my head! *(Suspenseful drumroll that crescendos like drums in TV shows when the lucky person is selected. A projected image of a wall of cell phones: dozens of white and black smartphones with cases in every color, some are broken, others are new, all have different lock screens. E-SMUGGLER chooses one of the phones, which fills the whole screen.)* I'm hearing over my earpiece that its code is 3570. *(He enters the code which activates the video. The telephone screen unlocks, we see the home screen photo and applications. We enter into this first woman's virtual world. Latin American music starts once we enter into the phone. We see the intimate world of her smartphone on the screen while E-SMUGGLER reviews her virtual life.)* It belongs to Anaba. In the Mayan language, that means, "She who comes back from the war."… Latin America, I love it… Beautiful pictures… Level 900 in Candy Crush, so she's pretty smart. She's Guatemalan and…a midwife! A sacred profession. Some professional apps:

While we see the apps on the screen, the PERCUSSIONIST makes an inventory.

THE PERCUSSIONIST: Breastfeeding Manual… Stop Blaming Women. Birthing Twins. After-Birth Reeducation. Perineal Meditation. That's interesting, Perineal Meditation… "Your perineum is a temple. Enter inside it, center yourself, and be in the moment."

E-SMUGGLER: That makes me think, we should improve our gynecological department for the migrants. They often encounter many difficulties: painful periods, pregnancy, giving birth, harassment… The poor things, they can't even find tampons while they're traveling.

THE PERCUSSIONIST: Other applications: Nutrition for the Pregnant Woman. Midwives' Testimonials. One hundred and twenty midwives were asked, "Why did you choose this profession?"

Lights shift, ANABA suddenly appears both on screen and on the stage. Simple and direct, like a close-up of the testimonial.

ANABA: To hear a newborn's first cry. To watch a woman seeing her child for the first time. To help her breastfeed, become a mother, to not be afraid. And of course…so women won't die in labor. *(Intimate film style with lights/sounds of the past. We also see her in close-up on the screen.)* I was 8 years old. My mother was pregnant with my little brother. I was born in Agua Roja, a village at the foot of a volcano. A very beautiful volcano. It's there, immense, we're afraid of it, we know it could erupt at any moment, but we still go on with our lives. We forget our fear and we live. We love it. In our churches, there are as many Mayan gods as virgins, which protect us from its anger. We don't want to anger any of the gods, we never know which ones are the strongest… Back then, there was no Internet. There was no road, no hospital, no school in the village. And no one spoke Spanish. That summer…nothing was growing. Not even the potatoes. We ate corn from morning till night. Every day. And as if that weren't enough to deal with…one night, it started to rumble. The volcano. A weird little noise at the beginning. The animals went crazy. Then a more and more terrifying sound, which came from the bowels of the earth. The neighbors started to shout…I remember…and suddenly, I heard my mother, "My water broke, go find Ximana!" The neighbor. She was the queen of childbirth, of wisdom teeth, of medicinal plants… I didn't know what it meant, "water broke." I went to go tell her my mother was going to give birth, but the neighbors were all panicked, running in every direction. The sky was purple. The birds were flying in circles. The animals were crying out. As if the whole earth was waiting for the birth of my little brother. I was shouting, shouting but nobody heard me. I went back to the house. My brother Wakiza was born that night. I saw everything. The umbilical cord, the placenta, the blood, everything… My mother cried… She said, "Even though I gave offerings to all the Mayan gods…it wasn't enough…" The volcano spat lava for three days straight. It made a column of ash. Very high. And my mother's uterus spat blood, for three days straight. No doctor came. Then she went up into the sky, with the volcano's ashes. I decided that day I would become a midwife. Wakiza grew up, and he became an angry boy.

While the image of ANABA fades from the screen, she whispers a Guatemalan song.

E-SMUGGLER: Great story! Facebook page. Hmmm… Lots of photos of births, babies… Two months ago, she posted another photo. Of her brother, Wakiza.

We see the photos on the Facebook page. A young man, in his thirties. In one of the pictures, WAKIZA looks like he's 15 years

ANABA: Wakiza, I found this old photo. Do you
remember? You spent your time trying to get in with the
soldiers. You brought them corn, coffee, you talked with
them, and when they started to relax, you would position
yourself next to their Jeep.

WAKIZA *(VOICE OF THE PERCUSSIONIST)*: To secretly
scratch the door with pieces of wood! Of course I
remember. I would prepare them in advance.

ANABA: Yeah, you had dozens of them. I kept them. I still
have a bunch in a drawer. You would whittle them. Good,
sharp pieces, to leave a fine line. *(They laugh.)* I would say
to the girls in the village, "My brother is so brave… That's
why my mother named him Wakiza. So that he would be a
warrior!"

WAKIZA: And then you would come home and yell at me,
"The whole village is going to be tortured because of you!"

ANABA: I was scared!

WAKIZA: It was all I could do against the army. With a
piece of wood, I felt like I was fighting against everyone
who had been killing us for the past five hundred years!

*(A pause. ANABA posts a photo of her free clinic on her
Facebook page. A simple hut. WAKIZA "likes" it. Comments*

appear on the screen.) The free clinic is finished? It's beautiful.

ANABA: Yeah, it's beautiful… We fought to build it, paint it, buy the supplies, collect the money. But it's useless. Everything is useless in this country.

WAKIZA: I miss the village. Post a photo of the volcano.

ANABA posts photos of the volcano.

ANABA: Look, it's beautiful today. The visibility is good. You always liked it when the summit was all purple. On days like that, I look at the volcano out the window of the birthing room, and I imagine you are there, just beyond the mountain. I wonder, "How does he live, what does he eat, where does he sleep?"

WAKIZA: Don't think about that. We're using our anger to kill people so that you can use yours for something else.

ANABA: *(dreamily)* Beyond the volcano, even further away, is Mexico. Then…the United States. San Francisco. You always liked San Francisco when you were a teenager. You would say that we would go together. Remember that song?

ANABA and WAKIZA sing a few bars of "San Francisco" by The Mamas and the Papas.

WAKIZA: Yeah. I would dream about that bridge. The Golden Gate. Like the one in Istanbul. I saw them in a film, they look alike. I don't know why, but I would dream

about those beautifully illuminated suspension bridges.
Maybe because the oppression of the Kurds made me
think of the oppression of the Mayans. It was
exactly…really exactly the same story.

ANABA: Remember? Ximana brought us two packages for
Christmas.

WAKIZA: Yeah, Ximana the midwife! *(He laughs.)* A blue
package for me and a pink package for you. A pistol and a
kit with a stethoscope.

They laugh like siblings do.

ANABA: I still wonder… I wonder what would have
happened if we had exchanged gifts.

WAKIZA: You would still be there, in your free clinic,
that's for sure. As for me, I don't know. Can you see me as
a doctor? Maybe I would have gone to school, instead of
learning to shoot and chant slogans.

They start to chant Guatemalan slogans.

E-SMUGGLER: A few days later… They had a WhatsApp
conversation.

*WhatsApp messages appear on the screen and mix with the other
images. WAKIZA's handsome face is speaking with his sister,
but the image is delayed. They talk, ANABA on stage and
WAKIZA's voice, which is not synchronized with the image.
The WhatsApp messages have Spanish sentences and emoticons:*

*smileys, flowers, angry faces, etc. THE PERCUSSIONIST is
still speaking WAKIZA's lines.*

ANABA: Waki, are you there?

WAKIZA: Yes.

ANABA: I'm leaving.

WAKIZA: What?

ANABA: I'm leaving.

WAKIZA: Where?

ANABA: San Francisco. Istanbul was too far, so I chose
San Francisco.

WAKIZA: Are you fucking kidding me?

ANABA: I'm serious.

WAKIZA: What are you going to do in San Francisco?

ANABA: I found a group of midwives on Facebook.
They're going to help me find work.

WAKIZA: You spent your whole life lecturing me! Saying
we had to stay, we had to fight for our country another
way. "Since you glorify death – fight with weapons – I
celebrate life – I'll fight with forceps – the women need me
here – so they won't die giving birth anymore…" And

now, you're telling me you're escaping? But you're right, of course they need you up there, those Americans!

ANABA: *(desperate)* I'm useless! I thought I could do something but no… They don't give us a chance. They want us to die. That's how it was when we were kids, and that's how it is now. They've been torturing us for decades. They won't let us speak our language, they sterilize our women, they burn our villages… But I thought I could still be useful. I still had hope. When they beat Papa in the village square in front of everybody, when they took our friends and we never saw them again, when you left saying you were joining the guerrilla army… In spite of all that, I always hung onto hope. I kept telling myself the general would be tried. The dictator would pay. For our women they raped, for our children they killed, our young people they hung. Our dead who didn't receive a burial. I was waiting for his trial. But he couldn't even be bothered to show up. They said he was too old to be present at the trial. *(On the screen, press clippings from Ríos Montt's trial.)* He won't even budge… He'll wait in the comfort of his home to be acquitted. That's when I realized… They'll never pay.

WAKIZA: Now you understand why I joined the guerrillas? It's because they'll never pay. We are always the ones who pay. It's the Mayans, the Afrikaners, the Uyghurs, the Aztecs, the Kurds who pay. You know what they did in Turkey? They gave five kilograms of bones to mothers who were looking for their sons, saying, "Here, bury these." And no one will judge General Evren there, or General Ríos Montt here! It's been centuries and the losers haven't changed.

ANABA: I'm lost, Waki, I don't believe in anything anymore. I've lost my strength. I want to live in a country where there's real justice.

WAKIZA: And you've chosen the United States as your country of justice. Bravo!

ANABA: Where do you want me to go?

WAKIZA: If you took up arms like me, at least you'd kill some of them!

ANABA: I don't know how to do that, Wakiza. I don't know how. I don't know how to kill. I've always done the opposite. Given life. (*Music. Lost in her memories.*) I leave tomorrow.

WAKIZA: How are you going to get to the United States?

ANABA goes towards a pile of coats and bags, she chooses a jacket, puts it on, then puts on a backpack. While E-SMUGGLER speaks, she crosses the room, carefully at first, then faster and faster. She jostles the audience, passes in between the seats, climbs on the backs of chairs, asks audience members for their hand to jump from one row to the next, etc. On the screen, we see a stream of images: the deadly Mexican border, close-ups of faces in extreme slow motion, alternated with others in a very staccato rhythm, and close-ups of WAKIZA and ANABA. Little by little everything speeds up. ANABA starts running through the theater, E-SMUGGLER speaks faster and faster, the images go by faster and faster, and the percussion becomes louder and louder.

E-SMUGGLER: *(a crazy patter, everything isn't necessarily intelligible given the infernal rhythm of the scene)* What? / What? / You want to know how Anaba did it? / With us, of course. / The Mexican border is one of the most deadly in the world! / Who other than e-smuggler.com could fight these formidable coyotes, the men who guard the borders? *(Here and there, THE PERCUSSIONIST speaks with him, as if he was chanting slogans.)* A twenty-million-dollar sale… / The most savage, ruthless, crazy, mean border guards. / On one side, American soldiers, on the other, the militia, not to mention the drug mafia, which doesn't think twice about transforming migrants into mules by making them swallow bags of drugs… / Without us, Anaba wouldn't have had a chance… / Without us, it is absolutely impossible to cross into the United States. Our men are with you every minute! *(While they spit out all this information, they unravel a string to create a finish line, like at a race. ANABA, out of breath, returns running to the stage. The tempo speeds up, she runs from upstage towards the audience and crosses the "finish line" like an athlete. The infernal rhythm stops. ANABA cries quietly. E-SMUGGLER is happy and satisfied. Calm returns. No more images, no more percussion.)* Oh, the moment where one of our clients, excuse me, migrants…crosses a border…you know, those moments where they still have one foot in one country and their other foot touches ground in their new country… That moment where despair becomes hope… For me, those are the most delicious moments I can imagine. It's…like an orgasm? Yes, there's no other way to put it, an orgasm. *(On the screen, cell phone images of feet positioned on lines. E-SMUGGLER returns to ANABA's cell phone. Several images of her journey, and a photo from the 1980s of open gift packages under a pine tree. Toys. In the blue package, a pistol. In the pink package, a doctor or nurse's kit. And ANABA's location on GPS.)* The location of her cell phone tells us she is at kilometer 2,423 of her trip. She just got into one of our trucks, en route to San Francisco! Also in her smartphone, her request for asylum, prepared and sent by our team. Because we also help you with your paperwork! *(He is back in "advertising mode." Jingle, images, lights, everything changes. We leave ANABA's world.)* I built this empire spanning thirty-three countries around the world, which is at your service seven days a week, twenty-four hours a day. I currently possess, as temporary lodging for all those who are fleeing, according to their budget:

E-SMUGGLER accompanies THE PERCUSSIONIST in his next monologue.

THE PERCUSSIONIST: Palaces, hotels, houses, apartments, studios, warehouses, and slums. And of course, trucks, vans, shipping boats, yachts, row boats, helicopters, cars, bicycles, and motorcycles everywhere in the world to carry you across borders. Thousands of salaried employees earn their living thanks to this multinational business: chauffeurs, pilots, soldiers, cops, customs officers, small-scale smugglers, medium-size and big time smugglers, merchants selling related products like life jackets, backpacks, cell phones, tablets, and of course special migration applications created by our I.T. geniuses! These applications show check point stats including how long the wait time is, tear gas usage, possibility of paying off the police at the border, how much to offer for a bribe, etc., all available on your cell phones.

Lights shift, images and costume elements change. A Vietnamese song. We see several cell phones on the screen. E-SMUGGLER is drawn to the telephone playing music. He looks in the phone, as do we, via the screen.

E-SMUGGLER: Hoa Mi. She's pretty in this picture. In this one, too. There. And there. Facebook account, "Paris Coiffure" in Hanoi. Specialty: Parisian Blowout. Brigitte Bardot Chignon. French Manucure. "Oh là là!" "Be as elegant as the Parisians." French songs. Vietnamese songs. This is the one she was singing. It's called "The Streets of Hanoi." Mmmm… "The Streets of Hanoi"…

HOA MI is in a Skype conversation with LÉO on her phone. The Skype image is projected, sometimes he's in the small Skype window, sometimes she is. The dialogue is lagging behind the image.

LÉO *(VOICE OF THE PERCUSSIONIST)*: "The Streets of Hanoi?"

HOA MI: "The Streets of Hanoi"…

LÉO: Sing another verse. *(She sings.)* What do the streets of Hanoi have?

HOA MI: There are so many people… The houses here are too small to live in, so we do everything on the sidewalk. We eat on the sidewalk, we relax on the sidewalk, we watch TV on the sidewalk, we chat on the sidewalk. Men shave, women wash their hair, kids do their homework on the sidewalk.

LÉO: What's your house like?

HOA MI: A ten-by-two-meter hallway without windows.
Four beds: mine, my daughter's, my mother's, and my
father's. I do everything on the sidewalk, too, laundry,
ironing, and cooking. And now I also do hair, since they
closed the salon.

LÉO: You style women's hair on the sidewalk?

HOA MI: Yes. I put out a bucket and a stool, I hung a
mirror on an electrical pole, and I do their hair there. But
it's not going to last. There's the mafia. They already came
by three times, threatening me to stop.

LÉO: Are you going to stop?

HOA MI: I can't. We have nothing to live on.

LÉO: What are you going to do?

HOA MI: I don't know.

LÉO: What if you came to style hair in France?

HOA MI: In France?

LÉO: You need money, right? I'll help you. I'll show you
Paris. I'll find you a job at a hairdresser's. If you work
hard, in a few months you'll go back to Hanoi with tons of
money. Hoa Mi, sing me "The Streets of Hanoi."

Music. Their conversation underscores E-SMUGGLER's monologue on virtual love that follows.

HOA MI: Paris?

LÉO: Yes, Hoa Mi. Paris.

HOA MI: Paris.

LÉO: *(correcting her accent)* Paris.

HOA MI: Paris.

LÉO: Paris.

HOA MI: Paris. Lio.

LÉO: Léo.

HOA MI: Lio.

LÉO: Léo.

HOA MI: Léo.

LÉO: Voilà, very good, Léo.

HOA MI: And mine isn't Oa Mi, it's Hoa Mi. Is it true that women say, "Oh là là!" in France? I saw that in a film, "Oh là là!"

LÉO: Oh là là!

HOA MI: Oh là là! Oh là là! Hoa… Hoa Mi. Oh là là…

E-SMUGGLER: Dozens of Skype conversations with Léo, over two months. Thousands of passionate messages: emails, WhatsApp, Messenger… Falling in love with an image on the Internet is magic! You aren't in love with the person since you've never seen them in real life, but you are in love with a new life that is possible with this person in your Skype window. In Facebook photos. In a Twitter timeline. In WhatsApp messages. This whole huge virtual part of love…which in reality doesn't exist because you have never touched the person, you've never smelled their scent, you've never tasted their lips, you've never really looked into their eyes, you've only ever looked at a point on your cell phone screen… This whole immense and virtual thing, you fill it with your dreams, your fantasies, your desires, and that makes you a migrant, it's marvelous… That which the imagination generates is always more beautiful than in real life. And then, to go meet your lover in flesh and blood, there's only one solution, e-smuggler.com!

Return to romantic atmosphere.

HOA MI: Hoa Mi.

LÉO: Oa Mi.

HOA MI: Oh là là!

LÉO: Oh là là! Oa Mi.

HOA MI: No, not Oa. Hoa. Hoa Mi.

LÉO: Hoa Mi.

HOA MI: Good! Hoa Mi means "nightingale."

LÉO: My little nightingale, sing "The Streets of Hanoi" for me. *(Music. On the screen, images from HOA MI's telephone superimpose as their calls multiply.)* Will you slip out of that?

With or without words, a strip tease on screen, to be improvised or worked out with the actors. HOA MI sings and finds herself half-naked while the words run together.

LÉO and E-SMUGGLER: *(whispering together)* Love / Paris / WhatsApp / Oh là là! / The women say, "Oh là là!" in France / Absence, presence / Love online / Take off your top / I'm saving this one / Message / Facebook / The present restored / Here and now / Your faraway movements / Movements of love / Travels / Skype / Hanoi / Paris / I am transporting you to me / My cell phone / Wait, I'm going to close the door to make love to you on the phone / Chignons / Money / Brigitte Bardot / The reproduction of love

HOA MI: I'll do chignons like Brigitte Bardot's in Paris?

LÉO: Girls like you earn a very nice living here, Hoa. They stay six months, then they go home with lots of money.

HOA MI: I know. There are whole villages here with nothing but men and children. The women have all left.

LÉO: You see? And when you return, you'll open your salon.

HOA MI: I'm buying my train ticket today.

LÉO: You need money for the plane. And for the preparations.

Accompanied by music from the live percussion, while images from the internet of Paris, Hanoi, and HOA MI mix on screen, E-SMUGGLER looks through the documents on her phone.

E-SMUGGLER: Afterwards, correspondence starts with a certain Li, one of our local smugglers. All the traces are in Hoa Mi's smartphone. She takes a large amount of money out of the bank: the date of the withdrawal. Then she borrows money: the number of the wire. The train, bus, and plane tickets… The fake passports for various borders she has to cross. But afterwards, Léo is no longer a bashful lover. He becomes who he is, a merciless man. Léo's last message:

LÉO's angry face on Skype in a montage cut with messages, photos, official papers, all superimposed on the screen.

LÉO *(VOICE OF THE PERCUSSIONIST)*: My little nightingale, you are starting to get on my nerves. You should have paid me the three thousand five hundred before leaving, and now you want to give me half once you get to Paris. I'm not going to get you here if I don't have the money, understand? There are hundreds of women waiting to take your place!

HOA MI goes to choose a coat from the pile, puts it on, then takes a backpack. She follows exactly the same border crossing

E-SMUGGLER: That moment… The moment where the
border is between a migrant's two legs. The moment
where she is on the threshold, on a line of demarcation, at
the edge of her life. The moment where we're between two
countries, two languages, two identities, two cultures! The
moment where this thing that is so abstract, that we call
the border, becomes a few grams of soil, a few liters of
water, a line of just a few centimeters. A customs office, a
check point in a war zone, a passport control area in an
airport, at a terminus, on a train track, on a road, in the
sea… That moment where despair becomes hope, the
moment where refugees who became zombies become
migrants again, hoping they will become human beings!
Yesssss, I love that moment!

*Same post-coital moment as after ANABA's border crossing…
The rhythm changes. HOA MI is on Skype in Paris, in a
different atmosphere than Hanoi. She has a large scar on her left
cheek. We see the face of a sad little girl in the Skype window.*

HOA MI: My darling! Can you see me? Yes, I see you. I
hear you. Tell the boy who runs the Internet café that he
should turn the video off if you lose the sound. Yes, I'm
wearing my hair down, now. No, I don't wear a chignon
anymore. How are you? Yes, Paris is beautiful. It's
beautiful. I don't get out much, but it must be beautiful.
There's six of us girls sharing the same ID card, so we
don't go out very often. I didn't call you before, my

darling, because I didn't have wifi. No, no, we don't eat French food. It's the Chinese neighborhood but we find everything here, Vietnamese, Thai, Cambodian… Are you working hard? How are grandma and grandpa? OK. I love you, my darling. *(Right before hanging up, all of a sudden in a stern voice.)* Promise me! Don't accept invitations from strangers on Facebook, OK? And get rid of that profile picture in that dress. Put up a decent picture! Do you understand?

HOA MI stays in her corner. The Vietnamese song and images of Belleville on one side overlap with the world of E-SMUGGLER.

E-SMUGGLER: Hoa Mi started a new life in Paris, thanks to e-smuggler.com.

We return to the melancholy world of HOA MI with the song "The Streets of Hanoi." She is dressed like a prostitute from Belleville, the Chinatown of Paris.

HOA MI: There are girls who have been here for a year, four years, six years. They all came for six months. All of them work for Léo. All of them told their husbands they were hairdressers, masseuses or aestheticians. Léo owns a massage parlor. We live in the rooms behind the salon. When we first arrived, we worked in the salon. It's more comfortable, better paid. We gave real massages. Californian, thirty euros. Thai, forty. There are also massages with a "happy ending." That's one hundred. Twenty for the girl, the rest for the salon. We do everything by hand. No blowjobs, no anal, no relationships, nothing. We don't wash the sheets, everything is paper. We throw everything away, after the "happy ending," it's practical. But later, when the girls are ruined, Léo puts them out on the street. And these are not the streets of Hanoi. It's hard. The Asians in Belleville are the cheapest prostitutes in all of France. Ten euros, fifteen max. Our clients are immigrants also. They don't have any money. Arabs, blacks. I had never seen them before coming here. There are some who are kind, but some are violent. One of them did this to me, on my left cheek. *(She lifts her hair, we see the wound.)* I can't wear chignons anymore. I hide my cheek with my hair. For the moment, I'm still at the salon. I'll leave before he puts me on the street. I'm afraid of the sidewalks. Of the street. Since I've been here, four girls have died. If he puts me on the street, I will go back to Hanoi. "The Streets of Hanoi." I just want to get my passport back. My passport. Then I'll go home. I won't see my daughter on Skype anymore. I'll see her in real life. I'll touch her, I'll kiss her, I'll smell her. I will really look into her eyes, not at a screen. I'll go home. I'll walk in the streets of Hanoi. I just want to get my passport back.

E-SMUGGLER: You understand, e-smuggler.com has a department for women who want to earn their living quickly and go back home. This department, which I've named happy-ending.com, grosses a revenue of three hundred billion in bitcoin. It's less risky than our drug department, because if you lose the merchandise in drug smuggling, it's a disaster. But if a boat full of women shipwrecks or is seized by the police, there are always other ways. As long as the world turns, there will always be women who need to travel to earn money. e-smuggler is here to satisfy men's desires and women's needs! Click

now for our rates and deals. Our prices right now are
unbeatable.

THE PERCUSSIONIST: Fifteen thousand for China-Italy,
twelve thousand for Iraq-Germany, nine thousand for
Cuba-America, twenty-five thousand for Pakistan-
England, and two thousand five hundred for Subsaharan
Africa-North Africa. And that's not to mention the not-to-
be missed opportunities thanks to cancellations, for
Cambodia-France and Afghanistan-Brazil.

*Arab song. E-SMUGGLER once again switches from intimate
mode to salesperson.*

E-SMUGGLER: Our European and American borders
obviously work extremely well. In the Aegean Sea alone
we have a profit margin of twelve million a month. Of
course, we think of everything. Our divers have placed
statues of the Virgin near the islands of Lesbos, Chios,
Leros, Kos, Samos, and Lemnos. Surrounded by tears, they
cry night and day for those who have lost their lives
wanting to cross the sea that was the cradle of European
civilization. And let us not forget the Korans we have
hidden almost everywhere along the coasts. We've also
thought of religion via cell phone: in real time, you are in
Buddhist temples at home, or at the Wailing Wall, or at
mosque on Friday, or at your neighborhood church on
Sunday! You know, my profession is a very old, sacred
profession. The first smuggler was Moses, if you think
about it. And you know what? I think, yes, I think that,
yes, yes, I should be a candidate for the Nobel Peace Prize!

Applause. Percussion, then darbuka and a switch to Arab rhythms.

THE PERCUSSIONIST: Ah, that Arabian rhythm… Of course, you've already guessed, we're now entering a smartphone from our hottest hotbed of volatility, which has been all over the news for the past seven years thanks to the Islamic Winter that followed the Arab Spring and multiplied our revenue by a thousand! There, it's no longer about migrants at all, but pure refugees! *(A beautiful Arab elegy. A more intimate tone settles over the acting, images, and sound.)* Mesopotamia has always been so fertile in exile, war, and conflicts that we have nonstop work. A land thousands of years old that the powerful have always washed with the blood of innocents. The cradle of civilization, which very soon may become civilization's grave?

E-SMUGGLER: And now…an Arabian telephone! Zeynab, a Syrian archeologist, has a phone filled with thousands of tweets from the rebellion.

Tweets in Arabic start to scroll down the screen.

THE PERCUSSIONIST: *(he chants in Arabic, in rhythm, while the Syrian tweets appear)* Come join us / Down with the tyrant / Cops soldiers assassins / Let's revolt / Government abdicate… / Down with Bashar! Down with El Doctor!

On screen, ZEYNAB films herself in selfie-mode at the edge of the water.

ZEYNAB: My Djihad, I hope you will be able to see this
video, and that they haven't cut off the wifi. I am trying to
speak as if…you were here, in front of me, but it's not
easy. *(She smiles.)* I'm in a warehouse. I sleep between the
anchovies and the red mullets. *(She moves the telephone to
show him.)* It's fine. Except that sometimes…I can't believe I
was so stupid, and I get so angry. I think you didn't have
the right to take such risks for a pile of rocks. And I never
should have left you. And then right afterwards, I
understand, I tell myself you are the most exceptional
person in the world, and I cry. Of course you should do
what you have to do. When you've finished your mission,
I will already be in London, waiting for you. And when I
see you there, I will make you pay for all this… *(She
laughs.)* Or maybe, peace will have returned, and I will be
back home, who knows? Our daughter? She's doing well. I
found a refrigerated truck…full of anchovies… *(She
laughs.)* Me, who hates anchovies… But I succeeded in
getting to central Anatolia in this truck, then in the
baggage hold of a bus, very close to the port where I'll take
the boat to Greece, just across the way. Those islands are
already Europe. Europe! Avroupa! I'm here, alongside
ancient Troy. Home of the great Homer. You used to recite
passages of *The Odyssey* by heart for me… I think you
would have loved to set off from here. Such poetry in this
misery! I'm determined to go see the ruins. I'll send you a
video on Wednesday if I have wifi. Take care of yourself.

DJIHAD *(VOICE OF THE PERCUSSIONIST)*: What a joy,
my Zeynab, a video of you! I kissed the screen of my
phone looking at you…at least twenty times. Even if it
smelled like anchovies… *(He laughs.)* My love, don't
worry, I will leave when the time is right. Not too early,

not too late. Not before getting the treasures into safety, burying this sarcophagus. I want this sarcophagus to bear witness. And not before taking care of the sculptures of these goddesses that no one believes in anymore, since they were replaced by one Allah. They're like that, they always break the statues of women first. They don't like women's bodies. They have a problem with… (*gestures to his crotch*). Don't worry, my Zeynab, I will leave before those psychotic destroyers get to the site. Time is flying, me and the other archeologists who've stayed are working day and night. There's only about ten of us. I'm thinking of you and telling myself soon we will be together. Together my Zeynab, my Zenobie, my Queen of Palmyra. We don't have cell service, and I don't know how much longer we'll have wifi. I love you, my Zeynab. (*Right before hanging up.*) Take care of yourself. And our daughter. On the road.

ZEYNAB's Facebook page. Photos of boats between Turkey and Greece: boat people, hundreds of life jackets for sale on the Turkish sidewalks, then abandoned on the beaches… A video of the sea, hostile and cold. Also a silly picture, where she's posing with an anchovy with a big smile. She writes a Facebook post.

ZEYNAB: On this page, there used to be my photos of my vacations, parties, concerts, barbecues with my Djihad, my friends, my family, and excavations. Now, it's…

Comments appear on her Facebook page while we hear them spoken aloud.

CHORUS: (*all actors taking turns with lines*) There's a boat leaving this afternoon / Are you taking the boat? / No, they don't take kids / I have two places in a van to the Bulgarian border / I'm taking the boat / It's a container ship / You have to get in the container / They make holes in the containers / I'm scared / No way / I'm not going in that boat / A dead baby traveled in this container for three days / The mother was Iraqi / The other passengers told her to throw the body into the sea but she didn't want to / The odor lingered / It doesn't go away / Unbearable / Pay attention to fingerprints / You must never leave fingerprints / You have to get rid of them / How / You scrape them against metal or you burn them with acid / But it grows back / The skin grows back / Do you have something to drink / Yes but it's for my son, he's sick / These life jackets are fake / ... *(Bottom of the water. Waves. A ship of refugees. Lights, sound, and video change. The characters are now on a boat. Water. The impression of being at the bottom of the water. Bodies and objects at the bottom of the water.)* I'm sick of the sea / Go on the other side / It's too heavy / Where's the captain? / Seventy-two of us on board / They said no more than thirty / That woman has a fever / No kids, I already said / You can't run with kids / There's a direct train afterwards / For the Balkans / From Greece / Do you speak French? / English? / Greek? / Turkish? / Albanian? / Pashto? / I'm thirsty / The sick woman is thirsty / That boat over there burst / They're in the water / Troy, is that it, Troy? / They're called Trojans / We're Trojans / The sarcophagus of weeping women / At the bottom of the water / Poseidon / Where are the mermaids? / Sing, O goddess, the anger of Achilles, odious anger that sent so many heroes' souls down into Hades / The border / There are also borders in the water / How are borders drawn in the water? / Are they drawn on the water or at the bottom of the water? / Ulysses / King of Ithaca / Hallucinations / Hunger / Thirst / Cold / Men go crazy /

Women go crazy / Leaving their bodies as prey for the birds, like for the dogs / The will of Zeus / Why are you leaving? / Because of the war / The bombings / We didn't have any more water / Even though we dug a well in the garden / When we knew they were coming / And you? / My family / Honor killing / That route is going to be hard / Very hard / They rape women on that route / No! / Yes! / No! / My husband already has two wives / Telemachus sets sail / To Pylos / Athena too / A fleet of twelve ships / Where are you going? / I have a cousin in Hamburg / My mother is in London / The gods will direct the winds / So that we arrive at the right port / If my brothers find me they'll kill me / I fled tradition / They saw I was no longer a virgin / We're here / The waves are cold / We're here!

On Google Maps, we see her route mapped out. The map appears on her Facebook page. She posts photos of a group walking in a forest. Below it, she writes: ALMOST IN HUNGARY!

ZEYNAB: The sea is over. The odyssey is complete. We've been walking for four days, we're walking and walking. And I'm thinking of you, my Djihad. And of the whole team. You must be exhausted. I'm doing fine. We're in Romania. I was sick on the boat, but I'm doing better now. And of course, I still have our daughter. I'm very tired, but when I think I will be in Hungary soon, I have hope again. Even if at night… It's hard. But… *(She laughs.)* The hardest part is that I feel like I can still smell anchovies! I bathe with very little water in rest stop bathrooms so the scent won't go away. *(WhatsApp messages appear.)* My Djihad!

DJIHAD: Don't shout "Djihad" in Europe, they'll put you in prison!

They laugh.

ZEYNAB: You're right, we can tell them we're fleeing executioners, but when you're named Djihad or Moustapha, they're convinced you're the Islamist!

DJIHAD: What's that thing you have on your head?

ZEYNAB: *(pulling down her veil)* Oh, it's nothing. Just something I put on so they leave me alone. *(Suddenly, she looks very homesick.)* Tell me, my love.

DJIHAD: We did it, the sarcophagus is safe, under a pile of bones. We covered everything up again with dirt.

ZEYNAB: So you're going to leave soon!

DJIHAB: I hope, my Zeynab, I hope so.

ZEYNAB: Hurry up, Djihad. They're saying the Turkish-Syrian border is only going to get more difficult. I'm afraid they're going to close it completely. Hurry, I'm begging you.

DJIHAD: Don't worry about me. Think about the long road ahead of you. Think of our little girl.

ZEYNAB: Yes.

DJIHAD: I miss you, my little anchovy salad!

ZEYNAB: After Hungary, they say everything is going to be easier. Then Germany and London. I'll find a job before you get there. Today, I wanted to eat something from home. It must be the baby, that's what's making me want to eat things from Alep'. Kibbehs, yalanji, baba ghanoush. They told me it's a pregnant woman thing. I downloaded a cooking app with the little bit of battery I had left. I was looking at pictures. I was dreaming…we were having a party. In that little restaurant you like in London. I told the baby you would be here soon. *(She rubs her belly.)* That we would have a party.

E-SMUGGLER opens the cooking app on the screen.

DJIHAD: A party…a very special party…

ZEYNAB: OK. But just so things are clear, I'm not going to be wearing a wedding gown.

DJIHAD: Did I just hear you asking me to marry you?

ZEYNAB: No way! You started it.

DJIHAD: Oh, really. I thought that was a marriage proposal, excuse me.

ZEYNAB: Why don't you make one?

DJIHAD: If you want… Do you want…? Why is it up to me to do it? You do it!

ZEYNAB: No, you!

DJIHAD: You.

ZEYNAB: You!

DJIHAD: No, you.

ZEYNAB: You first!

DJIHAD: *(in Arabic)* Will you marry me, my anchovy?

ZEYNAB: *(underscored with percussion)* YES, YES, YES! I will fly over the Hungarian border… I will walk like the ancient goddesses, tall and proud. *(Percussion stops.)* Djihad? Djihad? I lost you!

We see a cut telephone line on the screen. Images of European police, especially Hungarians, using gas and water cannons. ZEYNAB runs, the percussion picks up for the same border crossing sequence as the other two. She passes the Hungarian border while we see images of the police attacking migrants. Smoke. Percussion. E-SMUGGLER speaks with the vertiginous cadence he uses for each border crossing.

E-SMUGGLER: Zeynab flew over the borders of civilized Europe, and we followed her thanks to our drones! She found her way through European forests on Google Maps, and reserved her spot in "jungles," the refugee camps of beautiful Europe, cradle of civilization, where people are crammed in, mistreated, and poorly cared for. Sometimes, she mingled with people from the old continent, but regardless, Zeynab, an Arabian intellectual, was treated like an Islamist everywhere she went. That was part of crossing the European border. And she got there because she put her faith in e-smuggler.com!

When the smoke disperses, a message appears on her smartphone, full screen, "Hungarian Minister of Tourism: WELCOME TO HUNGARY!" The percussion slows down. The elegy returns. She gets up gently, coughs. Exhausted, she speaks.

ZEYNAB: *(speaking to her belly)* My Djihad stayed to get the sarcophagus into safety. He saved me. Your father was a hero. And he was so handsome. Indiana Jones but better. I remember the day when he discovered the sarcophagus…

DJIHAD: It was about ten years ago. I was the young head of excavations on an ancient site. Three kilometers away, there was a sort of hill that the villagers called "the hill of the assassinated girl." For two thousand years, if a girl dishonored her family, they would bring her there. Nobody knew why. And one day…it was hot, the work wasn't progressing…I decided to go see the hill. According to my calculations, I thought the necropolis we were looking for might be there. We started to dig. And under a cairn, we found this sarcophagus.

On the screen, we see the sides and frescoes of the Polyxene sarcophagus.

ZEYNAB: Scenes from the life of the deceased are sculpted on the sarcophagus. And there… There were scenes of an honor killing. It was the tomb of a young girl, whose throat was slit by her brothers and her father. We know the sarcophagus hadn't seen the light of day for two thousand years, but the oral tradition had been passed down from generation to generation… *(On the sarcophagus, a man with a knife in his hand next to a sacrificed girl. The girl is wearing a veil.)* My Djihad wanted to get the sarcophagus into safety. As a shameful object. As evidence. So we would understand what they do to women.

Percussion.

DJIHAD: Their descendants arrived. They destroyed everything with a macabre relish. They were so angry at everything that represented life, had such a desire to sack everything that represented beauty. They struck down grace. They ravaged the site. *(On the screen, images of Palmyra exploding. Strong percussion with each hammer blow that breaks a sculpture. Solo, then calm. It rains. Confetti? Raindrops? Seawater?)* Tell our daughter she should never give up her freedom. Her body's freedom. Tell her. Tell her, her father died for that. Tell her.

ZEYNAB: They don't like beauty. They don't like grace. They don't like childhood. They don't like freedom. They don't like statues. They don't like women's bodies. They don't like anything.

Black out.

E-SMUGGLER: From now on, we are in a world where no one has a house. We are all refugees. The only address that you have is your cell phone number. And from now on, I manage all two billion cell phones from my home. There are no more governments, no more United Nations, no more countries. Now I am the only powerful one. You cross oceans, lands, thresholds, borders, and all roads lead to my web site. I share in your journeys, your struggles, your joys, and your adventures. I have become the Lord of the Borders. I want to take this opportunity to thank all those who have inspired me since I was very young: arms dealers, statesmen, and businessmen, who have made it so that our planet has become a marvelous place where everyone can roam constantly due to conflicts and natural disasters.

Percussion solo.

Three Women

ANABA, HOA MI, and ZEYNAB on a TGV train. Percussion underscores the scene.

ANABA: These trains go fast.

HOA MI: Yes. Is this the first time you're taking the TGV?

ANABA: Yes.

HOA MI: Where are you going?

ANABA: To Hamburg. For a conference, on new methods of giving birth. And then to Istanbul.

HOA MI: Istanbul? Where's that?

ANABA: Yeah, Istanbul. It was my brother's last wish. I'm going to cross a bridge. And you?

HOA MI: I'm going back to my daughter. She's in Vietnam. I'm going to see her for the first time in four years.

ANABA: Four years?

HOA MI: Yes.

ZEYNAB screams.

ANABA: Someone's screaming.

HOA MI: A woman's scream.

ANABA: She's in the hallway.

HOA MI: On the floor.

ANABA: She's giving birth.

ZEYNAB: I don't have a passport… No passport. I don't want them to send me back!

ANABA: Let me through! I'm a midwife.

ZEYNAB: Tell the passengers not to call the police. I don't have papers.

ANABA: Don't think about that. Calm your breath!

ZEYNAB breathes deeply but quickly.

HOA MI: Breathe!

ANABA: I have my bag with me. Because of this conference. All my materials!

HOA MI: Really?

ANABA: You're lucky. Me too.

ZEYNAB: Why?

ANABA: How would you give birth if I wasn't here?

ZEYNAB: Yes, I get that part. But why are you lucky?

ANABA: I've always dreamed of this! Helping with an unexpected birth, that's every midwife's dream…

They laugh, then she cries out.

ZEYNAB: This hurts!

ANABA: Push!

HOA MI: Here, bite my shirt.

ANABA: Bring me some water!

HOA MI: I'll get it.

ANABA: Push!

ZEYNAB: I'm pushing!

ANABA: It's not easy, in a TGV going three hundred kilometers an hour!

HOA MI: Should I pull the alarm?

ZEYNAB: No! The police will come if the train stops!

ANABA: It's fine, you're almost there.

ZEYNAB: I'm afraid they're going to send me back.

HOA MI: Stop! No one will send you back!

ANABA: The head!

HOA MI: I see the head!

Percussion, the mother's cries, directions from the midwife, sounds of the passengers, the TGV, all get louder. The baby cries. Percussion stops.

ANABA: It's a boy.

HOA MI: He's handsome.

ZEYNAB: A boy? He's not missing anything?

ANABA: He's in perfect health.

ZEYNAB: He would have been so happy to see his son. He has his father's eyes.

HOA MI: Do you want me to call his father? Give me his number.

ZEYNAB: His father isn't here anymore.

HOA MI: I'm sorry.

ANABA: What's his name?

HOA MI: What are you going to call him?

ZEYNAB: I don't have a name for a boy.

ANABA: You thought it was going to be a girl?

ZEYNAB: Yes. What's on your cheek?

HOA MI: Nothing. A man did that to me in Paris.

ZEYNAB: It's the same mark the girl in the sarcophagus had.

ANABA: And the father?

HOA MI: Where is the father?

ZEYNAB: Dead. Dead back home. There where there are goddesses no one believes in anymore.

ANABA: You need to nurse the baby.

HOA MI: Can I call you by your first name?

ANABA: There you go. Just like that. Put your breast in his mouth.

HOA MI: Did he latch?

ZEYNAB: Yes. Arghhh…but it hurts.

ANABA: You don't know what to call him?

ZEYNAB: No. I want you to name my baby. You who welcomed him into the world. Give him a name.

ANABA: Call him…Akene.

ZEYNAB: Ake…?

ANABA: Akene. That's what my brother would have wanted.

HOA MI: Your brother?

ANABA: My brother. Dead back home. Far away. My mother named him Wakiza. That means "warrior," Wakiza. He said he wouldn't have been a warrior if my mother had named him Akene, "He who makes peace."

ZEYNAB: Akene. Thank you. And thank you, too.

ANABA: What's your name?

ZEYNAB: I'm Zeynab.

HOA MI: I'm Hoa Mi.

ANABA: And I'm Anaba.

Percussion. A Facebook page with a photo of the baby. Congratulations messages appear in every language.

End of play.

To my son, Ervan.
(Thank you, my son, for your close reading.)

CPSIA information can be obtained
at www.ICGtesting.com
Printed in the USA
LVHW031737050521
686579LV00005B/748